The Napping House

Audrey Wood   Don Wood

Harcourt Children's Books

Houghton Mifflin Harcourt New York

Requests for permission to make copies of any part
of the work should be submitted online
at www.harcourt.com/contact or mailed to
the following address: Permissions Department,
Houghton Mifflin Harcourt Publishing Company,
6277 Sea Harbor Drive, Orlando, Florida 32887-6777.

Harcourt Children's Books is an imprint of
Houghton Mifflin Harcourt Publishing Company.

www.hmhbooks.com

Library of Congress Cataloging-in-Publication Data
Wood, Audrey.
The napping house.
Summary: In this cumulative tale, a wakeful flea
atop a number of sleeping creatures causes a
commotion, with just one bite.
[1. Sleep—Fiction. 2. Fleas—Fiction.] I. Wood, Don.
1945— ill. II. Title.
PZ7.W846Na 1984 [E] 83-13035
ISBN 978-0-15-256708-8

UU TT SS RR QQ PP OO NN
Printed in Singapore

The original paintings were done in oil on pressed board.
The display type was set in EdPS Script.
The text type was set in OPTIAdrift.
Color separations by Bright Arts Ltd., Hong Kong
Printed and bound by Tien Wah Press, Singapore
Production supervision by Pascha Gerlinger
Original design by Dalia Hartman
Redesign by Jennifer Kelly and Michele Wetherbee

For Maegerine Thompson Brewer

There is a house,
a napping house,
where everyone is sleeping.

And in that house
there is a bed,
a cozy bed
in a napping house,
where everyone is sleeping.

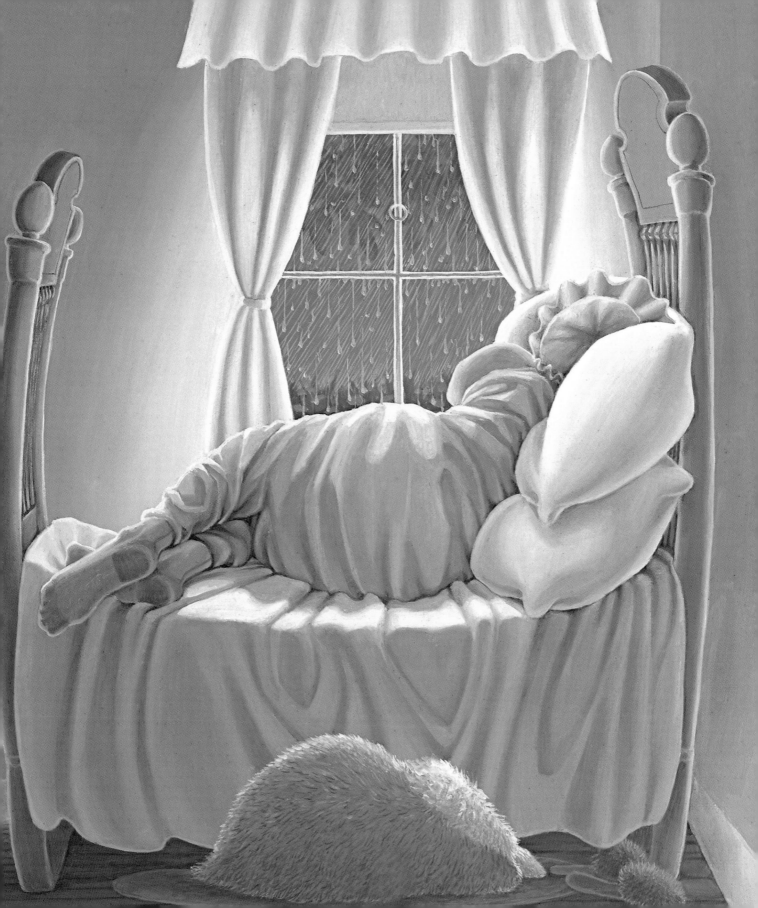

And on that bed
there is a granny,
a snoring granny
on a cozy bed
in a napping house,
where everyone is sleeping.

And on that granny
there is a child,
a dreaming child
on a snoring granny
on a cozy bed
in a napping house,
where everyone is sleeping.

And on that child
there is a dog,
a dozing dog
on a dreaming child
on a snoring granny
on a cozy bed
in a napping house,
where everyone is sleeping.

And on that dog
there is a cat,
a snoozing cat
on a dozing dog
on a dreaming child
on a snoring granny
on a cozy bed
in a napping house,
where everyone is sleeping.

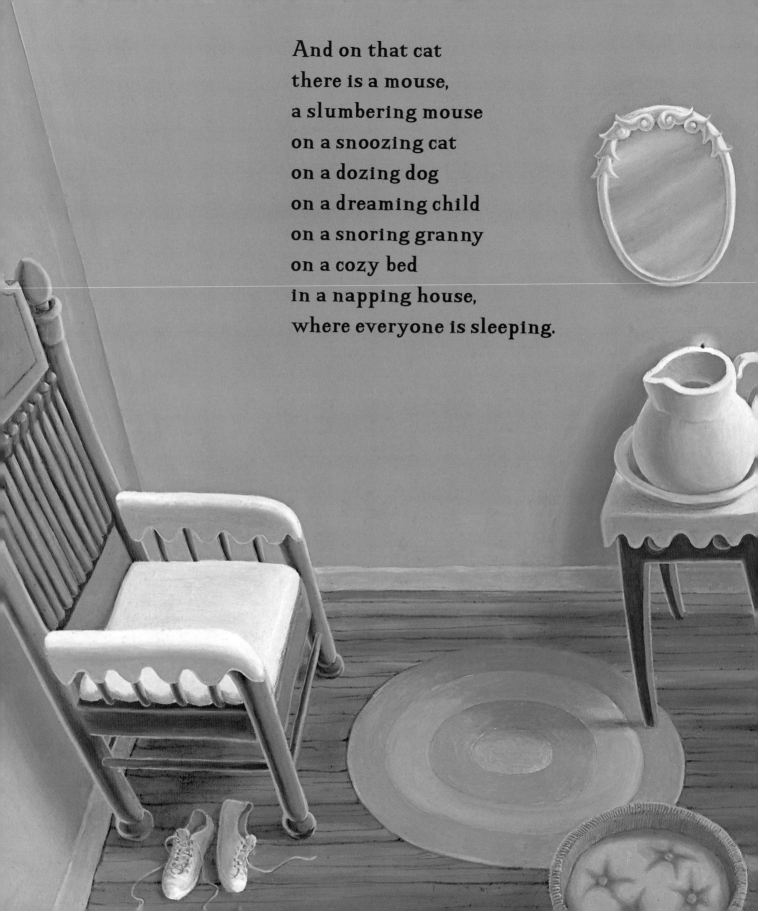

And on that cat
there is a mouse,
a slumbering mouse
on a snoozing cat
on a dozing dog
on a dreaming child
on a snoring granny
on a cozy bed
in a napping house,
where everyone is sleeping.

And on that mouse
there is a flea....

Can it be?
A wakeful flea
on a slumbering mouse
on a snoozing cat
on a dozing dog
on a dreaming child
on a snoring granny
on a cozy bed
in a napping house,
where everyone is sleeping.

A wakeful flea
who bites the mouse,

who scares the cat,

who claws the dog,

who thumps the child,

who bumps the granny,

who breaks the bed,

in the napping house,
where no one now is sleeping.